BIG JOHN TURKLE

For Ferd Monjo R.H.

For Diane M.B.

Text copyright © 1983 by Russell Hoban
Illustrations copyright © 1983 by Martin Baynton
All rights reserved, including the right to reproduce this
book or portions thereof in any form.
First published in the United States in 1984 by
Holt, Rinehart and Winston, 383 Madison Avenue,
New York, New York 10017.

Originally published in Great Britain by Walker Books Ltd.

Library of Congress Cataloging in Publication Data

Hoban, Russell.
Big John Turkle.

Summary: Big John Turkle, a turtle, finds his day
very unsatisfactory until he manages to make off with
boastful Grover Crow's newest treasure.
[1. Turtles—Fiction. 2. Crows—Fiction]
I. Baynton, Martin, ill. II. Title.
PZ7.H637Bh   1984   [E]   83-12661

ISBN: 0-03-069499-X

First American Edition

Printed in Italy
1 3 5 7 9 10 8 6 4 2

ISBN 0-03-069499-

BIG JOHN TURKLE

RUSSELL HOBAN

Illustrated by
MARTIN BAYNTON

HOLT, RINEHART AND WINSTON
NEW YORK

Big John Turkle was not having
a good day. Nothing was going right
for him. He'd almost caught a duck
but it got away.

Big John swam down
to his sulking place.
There he grumbled
and cursed and
sang his bother song:

'Bother here and bother there,
Too much bother everywhere.'

Big John began to think of lobster salad.
He had had some only once, part of a sandwich
dropped into the pond by a picnicker in a
rowboat. He thought of how it would be
to have a whole plate of lobster-salad
sandwiches to himself.

He swam up to the surface, then he swam slowly up and down the pond with just his head sticking up out of the water like a periscope.

The boat was hauled up on the bank and there were no picnickers to be seen anywhere. The sky was gray, the wind was riffling the water.

There were ducks on the pond, some of them were diving under the surface of the water, while others bobbed like boats at anchor.

Big John thought he
heard them laughing
as he swam past.

He climbed onto a
log that was leaning against
the bank. He listened to the wind
rattling the brown oak leaves.

Big John looked up and saw Grover
Crow flying backwards. He would fly up
into the wind and let it blow him back a
little way, then he would flap and flutter
down to the ground and hop around
chuckling to himself before
he flew up again.

'What are you laughing about?' asked Big John.

Grover Crow cocked his head to one side and looked at Big John. 'I've got a willow-pattern cup handle,' he said, 'and quite a bit of the cup as well. How about that?'

'Have you got any lobster salad?' asked Big John.

'Lobster salad is not an object of art,' said Grover Crow.

'Object of art!' said Big John. 'You don't know what life's all about!'

'Don't I!' said Grover Crow. 'Have *you* got a willow-pattern cup handle?'

'Flobbery!' said Big John. 'That's just a lot of flummery old flobbery.'

'You say that because you can't think of anything else to say,' said Grover Crow, 'and because you haven't got a willow-pattern cup handle.'

Big John slid into the water without a word, leaving a stream of angry bubbles behind him as he swam to the bottom. He tried to remember how the lobster salad had tasted but the taste would not come back to him.

    He swam up to the
surface again and saw Grover
Crow swaggering around with the
willow-pattern cup handle in his beak and
crooning to himself. Grover did not see Big John.
When he had finished parading with his art
object he carefully hid it under some dead leaves.
Then he flew off, laughing to himself.

'Flibbery,' said Big John.

As soon as Grover Crow was out of sight Big John hustled over to where the cup handle was hidden, uncovered it, and took it back to the pond with him.

Just before he slid into the water he looked up at the gray sky. The sky was looking wintery, it made him feel sleepy.

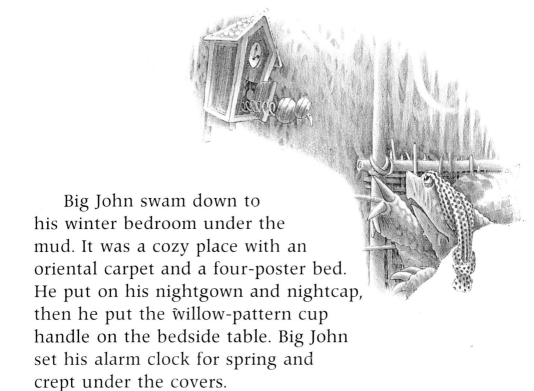

Big John swam down to
his winter bedroom under the
mud. It was a cozy place with an
oriental carpet and a four-poster bed.
He put on his nightgown and nightcap,
then he put the willow-pattern cup
handle on the bedside table. Big John
set his alarm clock for spring and
crept under the covers.

'Ahhhhh!' he sighed. He looked at the willow-pattern cup handle. 'Well,' he said, 'it isn't lobster salad but at least Grover Crow hasn't got it.'

Then he closed his eyes and with a smile on his face he went to sleep for the winter.